PAYBACK

GRAHAM MARKS

EDGE

FRANKLIN WATTS

LONDON·SYDNEY

First published in 2012
by Franklin Watts

Text © MarksWorks Ltd 2012
Cover design by Cathryn Gilbert

Franklin Watts
338 Euston Road
London NW1 3BH

Franklin Watts Australia
Level 17/207 Kent Street
Sydney, NSW 2000

A CIP catalogue record for this book
is available from the British Library.

donatas1205/Shutterstock: front cover bg.
Olivier Lantzendörffer/istockphoto: front cover t
pne/Shutterstock: front cover c.
vectomart/Shutterstock: front cover b.

ISBN: 978 1 4451 1442 2

1 3 5 7 9 10 8 6 4 2

Printed in Great Britain

Franklin Watts is a division of
Hachette Children's Books,
an Hachette UK company.
www.hachette.co.uk

*"When you get something for nothing,
you just haven't been billed for it yet."*

Franklin P. Jones

Contents

Chapter One

When Greg finally got himself up, everyone was out — his mum's scrawled note on the fridge said they'd "GONE 2 TESCO". That was odd because his mum usually did the shop on a Friday, and his dad liked to read his paper on a

Saturday morning. And they must have taken his little sister with them. Also odd, as she only liked going clothes shopping.

A quick check showed there was nothing much to eat in the kitchen. A more thorough search of the house came up with enough spare change for a fry-up at the cafe. Result!

Greg was on the bus before he realised he'd left his phone at home. It was up in his bedroom and still on charge.

Then the bus broke down, so
he had to walk the rest of the
way into town. And as these
things always came in threes, he
saw Barry Telford on the prowl
and had to take a major detour.
Bazz was someone even the
plague would try to avoid.

The safer route to town was via
various scuzzy backstreets and a
passageway, which was more of a
dog toilet. It took ages. So when
Greg finally got back on track, his
stomach was grumbling like crazy
and his mouth watering at the

thought of egg, bacon and chips.

He was about to cross the road when it felt like someone tapped him on the shoulder with a brick.

"Oi...Greg, innit?"

Greg looked round to see Bazz standing behind him, chewing gum with his mouth open, and lost his appetite.

"Gotta fag?"

"I don't smoke, Bazz."

"Lend us the money for one, then." Bazz put his hand out and wiggled fingers that were like sausages. It was his way of saying "Or else".

Greg had never heard of anyone saying no to Bazz and getting away with it. Which is why, without any money, Greg was now in the park — on his own and hungrier than ever. If he didn't think of somewhere to go where his friends might be, he'd end up wasting the whole morning.

11

He was hurrying down the path that led to the park gate, on his way to try his luck in town, when he saw a glint of light flash off something on one of the benches. Slowing down, Greg walked over and stared down at what looked to be a brand new, very expensive mobile phone.

Chapter Two

Greg looked round, trying to find the person who'd left the phone on the bench, but there was no one in sight. He was completely on his own, and right at that moment he realised that he couldn't hear a sound. There was absolute silence. No cars. No birds. It was like everything had just stopped.

A shiver ran down Greg's spine.

For some reason he remembered a movie he'd seen about the last man left alive, and it made him feel totally spooked. Then he looked back at the bench, half expecting to see the phone had gone, or that it was actually something entirely different. But it was still there, if anything even shinier than it had been.

Checking all around again, and once again seeing nobody, Greg sat down on the bench. The phone was easily within arm's reach.

It *had* to be a set-up. As soon as he touched the phone someone would burst out of a nearby bush and accuse him of stealing it. Or reveal that he was being filmed for some rubbish TV show. But then what if someone *had* just left it behind by accident?

Greg leant sideways and peered down at the phone, looking at it closely for the first time. It was, he now realised, actually just a thin oblong of mobile-sized black plastic, or maybe glass. It probably wasn't a phone at all. He shook his head, reached out and picked it up.

Whatever it was, it certainly wasn't made of plastic. The thing felt heavy for its size, and quite cold. Greg turned it over in his hands. He examined it from every angle to see if there was anything on the surface that would give him a clue as to what it was.

Nothing.

Not a mark. No brand name, no "on" button or headphone socket, nothing that looked like a way to open it up to change the battery or the SIM card.

He was about to put the object back on the bench and get on his way, when he felt something. It was as if what he was holding had...well, there was only one way to describe it: it was as though the object had woken up.

Greg stared at the black glass oblong in his hand, noticing for the first time that there were no finger marks anywhere on it...and that it should've been reflecting his face, but wasn't.

Then, right there in front of him, he saw a small part of the surface at the end nearest to him sink inwards to create a perfectly circular dip. It was about the size of a 5p coin, and it just cried out to be touched.

While Greg's mind tried to work out what to do next, his hand had no doubts. He watched as it moved towards the device, as though his fingers were remote controlled. And it didn't feel like his finger as it slowly, gently touched the dip in the polished black device.

"Hello," said a voice. "Good to meet you, Gregory..."

Chapter Three

Greg jumped up, like he'd been stung by a wasp, and glanced behind him. But there was no one there.

"Who?" he frowned. "Where?"

"You called," said the voice.

Greg froze. The voice was coming from the-thing-that-wasn't-a-phone, which he was still holding. He looked down at it to find that the black glass surface now looked like there was a drawing of an old-fashioned scythe etched into it.

"Not me...I didn't call anyone," Greg said. "Who are you — and how do you know my name?"

"I do apologise, how rude of me!

I'm Michael, but as we are going to be working together, you can call me Mike."

"Working together?" Greg looked round to see if there was anyone who might've heard him shouting. There wasn't. "What do you mean? I don't want a job — I'm at school!"

"Why don't you have a sit down?"

Mike's voice was very clear, making Greg feel like he was

actually standing right next to him. Confused, he did as he'd been asked and sat back down on the bench.

"What's going on?" Greg tried to put the phone down and realised he couldn't. Because his arm wouldn't move.

"You've been chosen," said Mike.

"Who by? For what?"

"Questions, questions!" Mike's

voice sounded like he was smiling. "You have been chosen by Fate, or quite possibly it might be Chance, although it may very well have been Luck. One or the other of those, anyway. And you have been chosen to be a Watcher."

"But I don't want to be a Watcher, whatever that is!"

"I'm afraid it's not your decision, Greg. The person who had the job before you came to the end of his contract, so to speak — by which I mean he died

— and the device was left here to see who would pick it up. You did. And so congratulations! The job is yours — unless, of course, someone else chooses to take it from you."

Greg opened his mouth, but didn't know what to say, so he closed it and slumped against the back of the bench. This was not how he'd planned to spend his Saturday afternoon, sitting on a park bench talking to someone who wasn't there when he should be off with his mates having fun!

"Don't you want to know what you have to do?"

"No!" Greg stuffed his hands in his jacket pockets and glowered at the world. And then he sat up straight and slowly took his right hand out. It was no longer holding the phone!

In a split second Greg was on his feet, tearing at his jacket which would not come off — no matter how hard he tried. He was about to have another go when he saw a woman with a buggy. She'd stopped a few metres down the path and was staring at him like he was mad.

"I thought I felt something." Greg made like he was brushing stuff off himself. "You know, like insects?"

The woman hurried past him without saying a word and disappeared out of the park.

"This is a job for life, Greg. Didn't I say that?"

Chapter Four

"Why me?" Greg kicked the bench, then he kicked an empty cola can, and finally he picked up a large stone and randomly hurled it. "What did I do?"

"You were curious," said Mike.

"And you were, like a jackdaw, attracted to the shiny and the bright."

"And now I always have to have this..." Greg gestured at his jacket pocket, "...with me?"

"Forever. Yes. Yes, you do."

"Why?"

"Because."

"That's not an answer!" Although he couldn't help feeling freaked out, Greg was also angry. He hated being told what to do, especially for no good reason. "Tell me what this is all about — now!"

"Very well." Mike, it was obvious, was not smiling any more. His voice had turned cold and steely. "I am one of the Reapers, a Collector of Souls, here since the birth of Life itself. We have never been able to be everywhere and have always needed human Watchers. They are our eyes in every corner of the Earth. You, Gregory, are now a part of an ancient and noble family."

"I'm already part of a family, I don't need another one — especially not a noble and ancient one, thanks very much!" Greg hissed, aware that he could now see more people in the park, and was in danger of being found talking to himself. "And what are you on about? What's a Reaper, and what does all that watching stuff actually mean? What do I have to do — and if this is a job, right, what do I get paid?"

"You are merely a conduit, a channel through which I see, that is all. You do not have to do anything. Through you I see who is ready to leave this life and move on, so I can be there. To help," Mike said, sounding quite enthusiastic. "And the job is its own reward, young man."

"I'll see people who are about to die?"

"Well, they are everywhere you look."

Greg was, once more, lost for words. Today — which had started as simply an odd day — had just got weirder and stranger and crazier by the minute. And now he was beginning to wonder if he hadn't actually gone mad, because how could any of this be true?

No matter how much he wanted to believe that if he pinched himself everything would be back to normal, in his jacket Greg could feel the weight (the phrase "dead weight" sprang into his

mind) of the device in his
pocket. It was there, and he
knew that what had happened
might be completely bizarro,
but it was real.

"It's not a bad job, Greg.
You'll get used to it, and one day
we'll get to meet."

"We will?"

"Of course!" said Mike. "One
day you'll look in the mirror, and
I'll know your time has come..."

Chapter Five

For half an hour or so Greg stayed
in the park, avoiding people as
much as possible. He'd started to
think that just looking at someone
might make them die. It took
him a while before he convinced
himself that he was being stupid.

He had a life to lead! He had a home to go to! He had friends he should try and link up with so he could forget what had happened. Because he knew what he really had to do was put all this behind him, and carry on as if nothing had happened. Otherwise... otherwise his life wouldn't be worth living, and he was not going to let that happen.

With his hands stuck in his jeans, Greg left the park and trudged his way back towards the centre of town. He didn't touch what was in his jacket, he kept his mouth shut and he ignored Mike.

It was not an easy or a pleasant journey.

On the one hand he tried to keep an eye out for any of his mates (he really could do with seeing a friendly face), but then he kept on seeing people who didn't look at all well. And not just old folks who you might expect to be about to "pop their clogs", as his dad liked to say.

There was the pale, bald man sitting at the bus stop, his head in his hands, quietly mumbling "No, no, no..." to himself. The very thin woman outside a doctor's surgery who looked like she was about to cry. The small child with the hacking cough...

By the time Greg reached the High Street he was as twitchy and nervous as a kitten in a kennel. And then to his relief he heard his name being called. It was Andy and Tim. They weren't his best mates but they would more than do, under the circumstances.

Greg waved, and instead of stopping, Andy and Tim carried on walking, beckoning him to cross over and join them. Greg was looking for a space in the traffic so he could cross the road. That's when he noticed the bloke who'd come and stood right next to him. He was waiting to cross as well.

There was something odd about the man. Greg couldn't work out what it was, except he made him feel sad when he looked at him.

"Well spotted, Greg! You're a natural."

Before Greg could react to what he'd just heard in his head, the man clutched his chest and crumpled forward like he was diving into the road. Greg instinctively reached out and caught the man's arm as he fell, pulling him on to the pavement. Greg knelt down, and stared at the man's face. The man stared back.

"Tell him it's going to be OK," said Mike.

Before Greg had a chance to think, the words were out of his mouth. As the man closed his eyes Greg thought he saw a wisp of something lift off him.

"You OK?"

Greg looked up to see Tim standing next to him.

"What happened?" said Tim. "You look like you've seen, you know, a ghost or something."

Chapter Six

Someone must have dialled 999,
as the next thing Greg knew there
were police and ambulance people
arriving from every direction. A
ring of bystanders watched and
whispered to each other.

Greg couldn't remember Tim
and Andy going, but he was on
his own, still kneeling next to the
body when a policewoman came
and moved him away gently.
She asked him some questions,
he answered them; she took his
name and address and then he
was on his own again.

Greg felt empty, but not hungry
in any way; empty and shocked
by what had happened, and all
too aware that it was not going to
be the last time he went through
this. As he stood, trying to think

straight, he remembered the jokey fridge magnet his dad had bought when they were away on some holiday or other. "Remember!" it said in happy, cartoon-style lettering. "Tomorrow is the first day of the rest of your life!" He'd never be able to look at it again.

"Cheer up." Mike sounded like he was smiling again. "You did a good job there."

"Terrific. Did I choose that man..." Greg muttered under his breath. "Did I kill him?"

"No, you just saw him. You recognised an end was coming, that's all. Remember, you're a Watcher, I'm the shepherd; we're a team."

"Oh really?" Greg sneered. "Where I come from you join teams. You have a choice."

"And you chose to pick up the device..."

With no money for his bus fare, Greg had to walk back home. He didn't care. He needed the time to sort out his head, to get used to the idea that he was going to be a Watcher for the rest of his life, and that there was absolutely nothing he could do about it. Would his family notice anything different about him? Surely someone was eventually going to notice that when he was around people tended to die? Mike told him not to worry, which was OK for him.

Later, thinking back, Greg would realise it was because he was worrying and fretting about the rest of his life, that for the second time that day he didn't see Barry Telford coming. Not until Bazz loomed in front of Greg and grabbed his arm.

"'Allo, Greg, mate," said Bazz.

"Um, hi, Bazz…"

"I'm a little short again. Need some bus fare, right?" Bazz held out his free hand, making his trademark "gimme, or else" gesture with his fingers.

"You've had all my money, Bazz," Greg said as he tried to work out what to do next; putting up a fight was not an option with the likes of Bazz.

"I'll have your phone then, me battery's flat…"

Before Greg could do or say anything Bazz had made a lunge for his jacket pocket. And then there Bazz was, looking at the shiny black device he now had in his hand.

"Very nice," he said, a big grin on his face. "How d'you make it work?"

As Greg stared at Bazz, Mike's words came back to him: "The job is yours," he'd said, "unless, of course, someone else chooses to take it from you." He could not believe his luck. Time for some payback.

"You press it," Greg said, watching as Bazz stabbed a sausage finger at the dip in the polished black surface.

"Hello," said Mike's voice.
"Good to meet you, Barry..."

About the author

I like to take myself off to exotic places on adventures, and often do so for the stories I write, like *Tokyo* (Japan, obviously), *Zoo* (California) and *I Spy* (Istanbul), but I also love the idea that the unknown, the dangerous and the weird can be found right where you live. You just have to be curious and look for it. To find out more about what happens in my head go to:

www.marksworks.co.uk

DEATHMIRE

JON MAYHEW

EDGE

If you enjoyed reading
PAYBACK, you might also like
DEATHMIRE, by Jon Mayhew.

Tom Striker is a mudlark, earning a crust foraging on the banks of the Thames for anything worth selling.

When his friend Billy goes missing, and he saves a man claiming to be Old Father Thames, Tom and his friends are caught up in a battle between powerful spirits.

www.jonmayhew.co.uk

Buy online at
www.franklinwatts.co.uk
978 1 4451 1466 8 paperback
978 1 4451 1469 9 eBook

Turn over to read an extract from
DEATHMIRE:

Tom stood, as helpless as Wilf, staring at the couple in the water.

Herbert was up to his waist in the filthy Thames, wrestling with Billy!

Only it wasn't Billy.

It looked like him but the skin was grey and dead. Billy's eyes glowed bulbous and black, much too big for his face. And his mouth curved in an upside-down grin full of green, needle teeth. He looked more fish than human, more dead than alive.

Herbert sobbed with terror, desperately trying to wade to shore and push Billy away at the same time.

"Help me," Herbert panted. Then with a gargling cry, he fell back into the water. The creature plunged after him with a hiss. The water frothed and bubbled as the two sank from sight, then all was still.

Tom looked at Wilf. The sound of someone scurrying across the muddy shoreline made them turn. It was Ophelia. She was pale and panting.

"Did you see?" she gasped. "Did you see it?"

"Where were you?" Tom snarled, turning his anger and sorrow on the girl, rather than trying to understand what he'd just seen. "You could've saved him!"

"I was just further up the shore," Ophelia said, frowning. "It weren't my fault. What could I have done? That...that thing was hideous!"

"He didn't stand a chance," Wilf whispered, his face drawn and white.

Tom looked down at his own trembling hands as he remembered the parting words of the old man.

"Old Jenny Greenteeth stole

my crown. She'll fill the river with her minions," he'd said.

Billy's teeth had been green, like rusty copper nails.

"I reckon we look for this old man I saw," Tom said, gently pulling at Wilf's sleeve. "He said he was Old Father Thames..."

"That old fool?" Ophelia spat. She glowered at Tom. "What will he know? He's barmy!"

"Well, what do you suggest?"

Tom felt his anger rising. "I've never seen nothing like that before. It ain't natural. You can sit an' wait for Billy to come back, but I'm going to find the old man. Come on, Wilf."

Tom dragged Wilf away and headed off to find Old Father Thames. Ophelia stood, arms folded, on the cold shore.

To find out what happened to Billy, and whether Old Father Thames can help, get hold of a copy of Deathmire today!